THE EDUCATION OF ADELINE

URSULA COX

1

The carriage ride to Hartfordshire Academy was long and uneventful, Adeline's heart pounding with anticipation and trepidation as she peered out at the rolling hills of greenery passing by. Her forehead was pressed against the cool glass of the window, fanning herself gently as the warm summer breeze caressed her cheeks. She wore a plain, yet fashionable muslin dress, her gloved fingers toying nervously with the lace at her wrists.

Upon arrival, her father, a stern man in a top hat and impeccably tailored suit, helped her down from the carriage, his gaze filled with pride and concern. "This is it, Adeline," he said, his voice hushed. "Your new home for the next year."

Hartfordshire Academy stood before them, a magnificent Georgian mansion looming large against the backdrop of trees and gardens. It was an intimidating sight for the young woman; its grey stone walls seemed to ooze power and secrecy.

Adeline followed her father up the stairs to the entrance, her heels clicking on the marble floors echoing through the hushed hallways. The smell of polished wood and beeswax filled her nostrils as they were led into the Headmaster's office. Sir Alfred Weatherington rose from his desk, a towering figure in his tailcoat and cravat, his eyes raking over her from head to toe. "Ms. Adeline," he said, his voice deep and commanding. "A pleasure to meet you."

Her father introduced them briefly before ushering her forward, and she felt her heart skip a beat when his large, calloused hand took hers, pulling her closer. "Your pupilage here will be demanding, but we guarantee exceptional results," he said, his eyes twinkling with expectation.

"I'm sure I'll do just fine, sir," Adeline replied, her voice trembling slightly. She wanted nothing more than to return home, but she knew this was her duty - to be prepared for marriage and society.

The Headmaster smiled, revealing a set of perfect white teeth. "I have no doubt of that," he said, his voice like velvet. And with that, he dismissed her father, leaving her alone with him. His hand lingered on her back as he guided her towards a door at the end of the hallway, the wood cool beneath her fingertips as she touched it. She could hear giggles and whispers from behind it, muffled by the heavy oak.

Sir Weatherington opened the door and pushed her inside, shutting it softly behind them.

Inside the room was a study, filled with leather-bound books and polished desks. But what caught her eye were the four women seated primly on the sofas and chairs, their heads bowed over their laps as they wrote furiously in ledgers. They looked up at her with eager eyes, their faces flushed and lips parted. One stood, bowing her head in respect.

"Adeline, dear," Sir Weatherington said, his voice taking on a sinister edge. "Allow me to introduce you to your teachers."

He gestured to each woman in turn: Madame Hughes, the Headmistress with delicate features and sharp green eyes; Miss

Evans, an impossibly thin woman with fingers like twigs that constantly traced over the pages of her ledger; Miss Carmichael, a plump redhead with rosy cheeks who constantly blushed as she spoke; and finally, Miss Thompson, whose dark eyes glinted mischievously. Each lady curtsied deeply before her, their skirts swishing around their ankles.

"They'll be teaching proper etiquette and all of the other things a proper lady of society should know. I will be teaching you other things."

His words sent shivers down her spine.

He turned to walk out, leaving her alone with these strangers. Adeline felt her heart pounding as she took a hesitant step forward, clutching her carpetbag tightly. Madame Hughes then spoke.

"Come with me, dear. I'll take you to your room where you'll meet the other girls."

They left the other three teachers and walked up the foreboding stairs and down a dark hall where Madame Hughes knocked and then quickly entered the room. The room was much larger than she had anticipated - at least twice the size of her father's drawing room - with ten beds neatly made up in two rows of five on either side of the room. Each bed was adorned with crisp pillowcases and clean sheets, smelling of lavender and fresh air. The walls were painted a soft cream color, accented by blue damask wallpaper. Sunlight streamed through the windows, casting long shadows across the polished wooden floors. There were nine other girls about Adeline's age sitting on various beds. Some were reading. Some were sewing. Some were chatting with each other quietly.

She took the empty bed at the end, setting her bag gently on the floor beside it. The springs creaked under her weight as she sat down, taking stock of her surroundings. The other girls continued their hushed conversations, whispering about who-knows-what.

The other girls in the room watched curiously. They exchanged glances before one of them spoke up, "Well, well, well, what have we here?" They giggled lightly among themselves while they waited for an answer from Madame Hughes, who gave them all a stern look before exiting with a soft 'goodnight'.

As soon as the door closed behind the Head Mistress, the whispers began again. "She's lovely isn't she?" One girl said as she admired Adeline from across the room.

"I can't wait to get my hands on her," another commented, her eyes bright with anticipation.

Adeline felt like they were a pack of wolves circling their prey, waiting for the perfect moment to strike.

"Welcome to Hartfordshire," a third girl said with a smile, walking over to her. She extended her hand, offering a greeting. "I'm Charlotte. You must be Adeline."

Adeline looked up at her with wide eyes, taking her hand warily. "Yes, I am," she replied softly.

"We're all excited to have you here," Charlotte continued, leading her over to the empty bed. "You'll learn so much here; manners, etiquette...and much more." She winked knowingly, causing another girl to snort with laughter.

"What do you mean 'more'?" Adeline asked nervously.

Charlotte leaned in close, her breath tickling Adeline's ear as she whispered, "You'll see... You'll see." The room was filled with the sounds of excited giggles and rustling of silk dresses.

Adeline shivered, wondering just what kind of school this really was.

Adeline unpacked her few things slowly, feeling the cool draft from the window against her skin. She couldn't help but notice how each girl was dressed differently; some in flowing silk gowns while others wore more modest muslin dresses. Beside her, one of the girls' breathing quickened as she watched Adeline unpack her corset and chemise. Adeline shuddered at the thought of having to wear such restrictive garments all day long.

As she laid out her clothes, she heard another girl chuckle under her breath, "You're going to need to loosen up, my dear. This place isn't like home."

Adeline shot her a nervous glance before returning to her task. Her fingers fumbled with the buttons on her shirtwaist, but she managed to change into a nightgown much more comfortable than what she was used to wearing back home.

A knock at the door made them all jump, and a young maid-servant entered bearing trays of tea and biscuits. She curtsied deeply as she placed them on a nearby table. "Madame Hughes sent these for you ladies," she said quietly before disappearing again.

The girls all got up and made their way over to the tray and poured themselves tea. Adeline followed suit and took a small sip - it was strong and bitter, but somehow familiar. She took another sip, savoring its warmth as it trickled down her throat. The biscuits were hard and crumbly, not unlike the ones her mother used to make.

After a while, the girls began to drift off one by one until only Adeline was left awake. The candlelight flickered softly, casting eerie shadows on the walls. As she listened to their soft breathing, a sense of loneliness washed over her. She stared out into the darkness, wondering what tomorrow would bring...

Suddenly, there was a sharp gust of wind that rattled the windowpane, causing one of the other girls to whimper softly in her sleep. Adeline's heart raced briefly before she tried to calm herself with deep breaths. The moon's light cast an ethereal glow over everything, making everything seem surreal. The sound of distant thunder rolled in from outside.

The sound of footsteps echoed in the hallway, causing everyone to stir slightly. It was Madame Hughes, checking on them before retiring to her own quarters. She walked over to Adeline, smelling of lavender and lemon verbena, her robes flowing elegantly around her feet. "Sleep well," she whispered softly before extinguishing the candles one by one until only a single flicker remained.

With the last candle gone, darkness consumed the room completely. Adeline felt the softness of her blankets, pulling them up to her chin as she tried to get comfortable on the hard mattress. The silence was deafening now, only broken by the rhythmic breathing of her new companions. She couldn't help but wonder what sort of place she had gotten herself into - this academy felt more like a prison than a school.

She tried to fall asleep but found it impossible. Every sound seemed amplified in the stillness; every creak of the floorboards, every flutter of curtains, every snore from the other girls. Just as she thought she might go insane from the silence, she heard foot-steps approaching down the hallway again. It was much louder this time, accompanied by muffled whispers and giggles. Fear gripped her heart as she listened intently. The door opened slowly, revealing a hooded figure carrying a lantern that cast eerie shadows on the walls.

The figure approached her bed, stopping right beside her. Adeline couldn't move or scream, paralyzed with fear. As the hood dropped to reveal Sir Alfred Weatherington's lecherous grin, she knew something was about to happen. He climbed onto her bed and began to partially undress, his eyes never leaving hers as he did so. His skin was pale and slick with sweat under the dim light of the lantern.

His hands were cold as they touched her, making her shiver uncontrollably. He pulled back the covers slowly, inching closer to her quivering body. She could taste bile rising up in her throat as she tried to scream but nothing came out. And then he kissed her neck, his cold lips sending shivers down her spine.

"Welcome to Hartfordshire Academy, my dear," he whispered against her skin. "You're going to be the most interesting pupil yet."

As he traced circles around her nipples with his fingertips, Adeline felt a strange tingling sensation spread through her body - something akin to excitement mixed with terror. She tried to fight it but couldn't seem to move. His touch was unlike anything she had ever felt before; it was almost as if he were branding her skin with his desire.

His hands moved lower, down to her thighs where he slipped his cold fingers between her legs. She gasped as they touched her, causing him to chuckle darkly. He continued his exploration, teasing her clitoris until she squirmed under his touch. It was then that she realized what he was doing - touching himself while touching her.

She tried to push him away, but it was no use. He held her down with ease, his strength overpowering hers. He moaned loudly into the darkness and came, his hot seed soaking through her nightgown and seeping into her skin. The feeling was revolting yet strangely exhilarating.

Sir Alfred got off of her, leaving a trail of cold air in his wake as he pulled the covers back up and smoothed them over her trembling form. He leaned in close once again, his breath hot on her ear. "This is just the beginning, my dear," he whispered. "Tomorrow you'll begin your real training here at Hartfordshire."

With that, he blew out the lantern and left the room, leaving Adeline alone in the darkness with her thoughts and newfound fears about what was to come.

2

As the first light of dawn filtered through the curtains of Hartfordshire Academy, Adeline awoke with a start. Her heart pounded within her chest, and she felt as though a fog of confusion and violation swirled around her. As she sat up in bed, she noticed her once pristine nightgown now stained with the evidence of Sir Alfred's visit during the night. Her cheeks flushed crimson, and she hastily hid the soiled garment beneath her mattress.

"Good morning, Adeline," called a voice from across the room. It was Charlotte. She wore a coy smile on her face as she watched Adeline struggle to compose herself.

"Good... good morning," stammered Adeline, attempting to feign normalcy. Inside her mind, however, questions surged like an untamed river, threatening to drown her with their intensity. How could this have happened? What would become of her?

"Adeline, dear, it's time to get dressed for breakfast," Mary, another girl from the academy, chimed in. Her voice seemed to echo the same knowing tone as Charlotte's.

With trembling hands, Adeline donned her day dress, feeling

exposed even while clothed. As she made her way toward the dining hall, she felt the weight of the other girls' gazes upon her. Their whispers and snickers seemed to swirl around her like a sinister breeze, chilling her to the core.

"Did you enjoy your evening, Adeline?" one girl whispered to another, barely stifling her laughter. "I remember my first time with Sir Alfred..."

"Shush, she'll hear you!" the other girl hissed back, casting a glance in Adeline's direction. "Besides, she has no idea yet what awaits her."

Adeline's breath caught in her throat as she listened to their words. The truth was, she had no idea what awaited her. But the gleeful malice in the other girls' voices made her heart sink, and a sick feeling of dread curled up within her stomach.

"Come now, Adeline," Charlotte said, looping her arm through Adeline's as they entered the dining hall. "You mustn't let them get to you. They've all been where you are now."

"Then why... why do they mock me so?" Adeline asked, her voice barely audible.

"Tradition" Mary whispered from behind them.

With those words ringing in her ears, Adeline sat down for breakfast, her appetite gone but her mind racing with the possibilities of what was yet to come.

The dining hall was filled with the usual clatter of cutlery and chatter, but Adeline couldn't focus on her food. Her mind was elsewhere, lost in the memories of last night. She could feel eyes on her, feel the weight of their stares. She could hear whispers about her, but she couldn't make out the words. The smell of freshly brewed coffee and toast only served to remind her of Sir Alfred's musky scent from the previous evening. Every so often, she caught sight of his gaze on her, intense and predatory.

Finally, the meal came to an end, and they all filed out of the hall to line up for their next class. She stood at the front of the queue, waiting for Sir Alfred to appear. He did so with a smirk on his face, taking his time. She tried to maintain her composure, but inside she was trembling. He walked up to her, his hand brushing against her thigh as he passed by. It felt like an electric shock. He leaned in close, his warm breath against her ear. "Are you ready for your first lesson?" he purred.

Adeline swallowed hard. "Lesson?" She asked, her voice barely above a whisper.

"Oh, yes, my dear," he replied, his hand squeezing her ass tightly. "You're going to learn everything you need to know about being a woman." His words sent a shiver down her spine.

She was led to his office, heart racing. The door closed behind them, and she was alone with him once again.

Suddenly, the door opened, and Madame Hughes walked in. Her stern face softened as she looked at Adeline, and she gestured for her to follow. They walked down the hall to a room labeled 'medical', where they were greeted by a doctor and a nurse. The doctor was an older gentleman with a kindly face, but there was something unsettling about the look in his eyes as he examined her. He asked her to remove her clothes, taking note of every inch of her body, feeling her up in ways that made her blush.

"This," he said, running a finger down the crack of her ass. "Tell me if anything feels painful or unusual." His voice was deep and commanding.

Adeline's cheeks reddened as she shook her head. "Nothing...sir."

"Good, good," he replied. "Now turn around."

She did as she was told, biting her lip as he ran his hands across her stomach and chest, cupping her breasts in his large hands. Her nipples hardened at his touch, and she let out a soft moan. She couldn't believe how good it felt.

Next, he examined her sex, his fingers sliding into her wetness. She gasped at the intrusion, her hips bucking off the table unconsciously. The nurse watched closely, taking notes as the doctor continued to probe and examine. With each touch, she felt a surge of pleasure course through her body, making her writhe beneath his fingers. It was all so confusing— one part of her hated what was happening, but another part was enjoying the sensations too much. The headmaster watched silently from the corner of the room, a smirk playing on his lips as he observed their interaction.

Finally, after what felt like an eternity, the doctor finished and stepped back, nodding at Sir Alfred. "She's clean," he announced. "No signs of harm done."

Sir Alfred nodded grimly. "Good. I'll take it from here." He walked over to her, his eyes roaming over her naked form while the doctor and nurse quickly left the room.

"I-I don't know what you want me to do," Adeline stammered nervously.

"You just relax," he said, his voice a low rumble. He positioned himself between her legs and began to kiss and lick her most intimate places. His tongue danced around her clit, sending waves of pleasure through her body. She gasped and writhed under his touch, arching her back as he teased her mercilessly. She couldn't believe how good it felt—but also how shameful.

As he worked his magic, he whispered dirty words of encouragement in her ear, making her blush even more deeply than before. "That's it, Adeline. Let go. Let me show you what pleasure feels like. Come for me. Come, Adeline!"

She closed her eyes, focusing on the sensations washing over her body. She had no idea what he meant when he told her to come, but she knew that what he was doing felt incredible. The wetness between her legs grew as his tongue circled her clit faster and faster until she couldn't stand it anymore. With a cry of release, she came hard in his mouth, her hips bucking up off the table as he lapped greedily at her juices.

When he finally pulled away, Adeline was dizzy with pleasure and arousal. She looked into his eyes, feeling both exhilarated and embarrassed by what had just transpired. This act felt wrong yet so incredibly right at the same time.

"Good girl," Sir Alfred said as he stood up and looked at her.

"You just had your first orgasm. This is just the beginning of a world of unbelievable pleasure that you are going to learn while here at Hartfordshire."

"Now get dressed and go finish your other lessons with the girls."

Sir Alfred left the room and Adeline sat there in stunned silence. She had no idea what was happening, but she knew that she was both excited and terrified by it.

3

Over the next few days, the halls of Hartfordshire Academy echoed with the sound of laughter and rustling crinoline skirts. Adeline, her cheeks flushed with the rosy hue of innocent curiosity, listened attentively to her instructors as they provided lessons on etiquette, embroidery, and the art of conversation. The bright sun shone through the tall windows, casting light on the delicate fingers of the young ladies as they practiced their needlework.

"Remember to keep your posture straight, ladies," the instructor, Miss Evans, said firmly. "A lady must always maintain an air of dignity and grace."

Adeline nodded quietly, her thoughts occasionally drifting towards Sir Alfred. She couldn't help but notice that every so often, he would summon one or more of the other girls for what he called "private instruction." When they returned, they seemed both exhausted and strangely content, their cheeks glowing with a warmth she couldn't quite decipher. Curiosity gnawed at her, but she dared not ask any questions.

"Adeline, can you please demonstrate the proper way to pour tea?" Miss Evans asked, pulling her from her reverie.

"Of course, Miss Evans," Adeline replied, standing up gracefully. She glided to the table where an ornate silver teapot sat, filled with steaming liquid. Lifting the pot with a steady hand, Adeline carefully poured the hot tea into a delicate porcelain cup, ensuring not a single drop was spilled.

"Very well done, Adeline," Miss Evans praised, causing a small smile to light up the young woman's face.

"Thank you, Miss Evans," Adeline murmured, feeling a burst of pride in her chest.

As the day wore on, Adeline couldn't help but continue to observe Sir Alfred from afar. What exactly were these private instructions he was giving, and why hadn't she been chosen for any? The questions swirled through her mind, mingling with the intoxicating aroma of fresh flowers that filled the academy.

"Adeline, are you paying attention?" Miss Evans's stern voice snapped her from her thoughts yet again.

"Apologies, Miss Evans," Adeline replied, shaking her head to clear it. She focused her attention back on the lesson at hand, vowing to herself not to let her curiosity get the better of her. But as the sun dipped lower in the sky and the shadows lengthened, she wondered what mysteries lay behind Sir Alfred's closed door, and when, if ever, she would find out for herself.

Finally, as the final bell rang, signaling the end of classes for the day, Adeline found herself alone in the hallway outside Sir Alfred's office. She lingered there, her heart thumping wildly against her chest as she tried to listen through the door.

"Adeline," his deep, commanding voice called out from within the room, making her jump. Her cheeks flushing with embarrassment at being caught eavesdropping, she timidly entered at his beckoning.

"Adeline. What do you think you are doing?" he said, looking up from his desk. "Eavesdropping is strictly forbidden. You are supposed to be in your room with the other girls. What do you have to say for yourself?"

"I, I, am so sorry," Adeline sputtered. "I didn't mean..."

"Enough!" Sir Alfred shouted. "You have broken a very serious rule and must be punished. Take off your clothes."

"What are you waiting for? Remove them!"

Adeline started removing her clothes immediately. She was terrified but also incredibly aroused.

She stood there in front of Sir Alfred while he looked at her sternly.

He suddenly stood up and walked over to her. His warm breath fanned across her neck, sending shivers down her spine. She swallowed hard as he guided her over to a large leather chair in the corner of the room and instructed her to sit.

As she did as she was told, her heart pounded in anticipation. A cool, metallic object was pressed into her palm - a feather duster. Her eyes widened in confusion, but she didn't dare ask questions under the intense gaze he fixed upon her.

"Spank yourself," he commanded gruffly.

She hesitated for only a moment before doing as she was told, her hand hovering over her plump bottom. The cool feathers tickled at first as they brushed against her flesh but soon became a fiery sting as she began to strike herself. Each smack echoed through the otherwise silent room, growing louder and more intense with each strike.

"Harder," he ordered, his voice thick with lust.

Adeline complied, slapping her bottom harder until it felt like it was on fire. Her breath quickened as the sting turned into a burning desire, and she could feel the heat between her legs growing with each smack.

Her bottom was already sore from the first spanking, but she didn't dare protest or stop until he finally stopped her. "That's it," he murmured approvingly.

Next, he produced a bottle of oil from his desk drawer and instructed her to rub it onto her sore bottom. The cold, slippery substance made her gasp as it coated her palm and then slid down her thighs.

Shakily, she reached back and began to massage the oil onto her reddened skin, her fingers gliding effortlessly across the hot, sensitive flesh. The scent of his cologne filled the air as he stepped closer, placing his hands on her shoulders, guiding her movements.

"That's it," he breathed. "Now lie down."

Adeline complied, her heart racing as she rested on her belly on the chair, presenting her abused behind to him. She gasped as he began to lick and nibble at the sore surface, tasting the mix of oil and her flesh. "Oh, God," she moaned, arching her back to give him better access.

Her breathing was ragged now as he continued his ministrations, his tongue going deeper and teasing her opening. She could feel herself getting wetter by the second, her hips bucking against his mouth. Soon, he pressed a finger inside her, filling her with a deep, aching need.

"You're so wet," he rasped against her skin.

"Please, Sir..." She couldn't finish her sentence before he two fingers into her tight pussy.

"You are so tight. Are you ready for my cock? Do you think you could handle this inside your pussy?"

Sir Alfred suddenly dropped his trousers and was holding a very large cock in his hands.

Adeline had never seen such a thing. It was huge and hard and red. She had no idea how to respond.

"You aren't ready for that yet, but it won't be long," Alfred said.

Adeline was in a haze of desire and confusion. She didn't know what to say or do.

"Get down on your knees," Alfred ordered her.

Adeline did as she was told.

"Now, I want you to look at my cock. Touch it."

Adeline gripped the hard shaft with her small fingers. In the grip of her hand, it looked even larger than it had moments earlier. The head was swollen and pulsing and she felt a sudden urge to put it in her mouth.

"That's right," he groaned. "Get it all wet."

She took the head into her mouth and ran her tongue around the tip. She could feel him growing even harder and longer.

"That's it. Now show me how you suck that cock." She obliged, taking as much of it into her mouth as she could.

"That's beautiful," he murmured, his hands in her hair.

Her lips wrapped around his shaft, she began to bob her head up and down. She was lost in the feeling of his cock throbbing against her tongue, the salty taste of it coating her tongue.

"I want you to swallow my cum," Alfred ordered.

Adeline was too far gone to object. Her mouth full of him, her cheeks flushed.

Alfred grabbed the back of her head and guided her up and down on his cock until he suddenly let out a low groan.

"Swallow it all," he commanded.

Adeline obeyed. She drained every last drop of his cum.

"Good girl," he said with a smile. "You have a natural talent with your mouth. I think you will fit in just fine here."

"Thank you, Sir," Adeline said, staring at his cock.

"Now, do you want to come too? Are you going to be a good girl?"

"Yes, sir. I'll be a good girl," Adeline replied.

"Lay back on the sofa," Alfred commanded.

"Yes, sir."

Sir Alfred spread Adeline's legs and began exploring her slick, wet pussy with his tongue.

She moaned as his tongue slid over her folds, teasing her clit.

"That's right, you want more, don't you? You want my tongue inside you?"

"Yes, sir," Adeline moaned.

He plunged his tongue into her hot, wet hole. She could feel herself getting closer and closer to a shattering orgasm with each flick of his tongue. Her whole body began to tingle, her toes curling.

"Please, sir," she moaned. "I'm close, I'm so close..."

"I want you to cum for me, little slut," he whispered as his tongue slid in and out.

"I want that sweet little pussy to cum all over my tongue."

Adeline could hold back no longer. Her body stiffened as she came, her fingers gripping her hair. Her moans filled the room as she rode out her orgasm, the waves of pleasure rolling through her with each pump of his tongue.

"Good girl, Adeline. You are one of my best students. It won't be long until you are ready for me to put my cock in you. Do you want that? Do you want me to put my huge cock in your tight pussy?"

"Yes, sir. I want your cock badly."

The words that were coming out of Adeline's mouth were both foreign to her and wildly natural. She had no idea who she was anymore, but she knew she would never be the same.

"Soon, Adeline. Soon. For now, you must get dressed and go back to your room."

4

The next day, a soft, golden light filtered through the conservatory windows, casting a warm glow on Adeline and her newfound friends. They sat in a close circle on plush upholstered chairs, their laughter filling the air as they shared stories of their time at Hartfordshire Academy.

"Remember when Lady Emmeline accidentally spilled ink all over her dress during calligraphy lessons?" Eliza giggled, causing the others to burst into laughter as well.

"Ah, yes! She looked like she'd been attacked by an octopus!" Catherine chimed in, holding her sides from laughing so hard.

Adeline couldn't help but smile at the camaraderie that had blossomed between her and the other girls. Initially, she had been met with skeptical glances and whispers behind her back, but now, she was truly one of them. Her heart swelled with gratitude for the genuine connections she had made.

"Speaking of lessons," began Amelia, her hazel eyes twinkling mischievously. "We've noticed you've been spending quite a bit of time with Sir Alfred during your private study sessions. Are you enjoying your lessons with him?"

A rosy hue crept up Adeline's cheeks as she thought back to her intimate encounters with the headmaster. "Yes," she admitted, her voice barely above a whisper. "I find his teachings most... enlightening."

"Enlightening, you say?" Eliza raised a curious eyebrow, leaning forward with interest. "Do tell us more, dear Adeline."

"Sir Alfred has shown me aspects of life I never knew existed," Adeline confessed, her fingers nervously fiddling with the lace trim of her skirt. "He has opened my mind and my body to new sensations and experiences. I only wish our lessons could be closer together, for there is so much to learn."

"Indeed, Sir Alfred is known for his unique teaching methods," Catherine murmured, a knowing smile playing on her lips.

"His lessons have certainly brought us all closer together, haven't they?" Amelia added, her gaze lingering on Adeline with a warmth that sent a shiver down her spine.

As the sun dipped lower in the sky and the shadows lengthened across the conservatory floor, Adeline felt an overwhelming sense of belonging. These girls, once strangers, had now become her closest confidantes and allies. Together, they navigated the uncharted waters of womanhood under Sir Alfred's expert guidance, each one longing for more knowledge and deeper connections.

"Adeline," Eliza whispered, her eyes filled with sincerity. "We are so glad you're here with us. We're all in this journey together."

And for the first time since arriving at Hartfordshire Academy, Adeline truly believed it.

The sun cast a warm, golden glow over the conservatory as Adeline and her newfound friends lounged amongst the plush cushions and intricately woven rugs. Their laughter filled the air, mingling with the sweet scent of blooming roses just outside the open windows. Gone were the days of whispered secrets and stolen glances; these girls now shared their deepest thoughts and desires openly with one another.

"You know, Adeline, you don't have to have Sir Alfred to make you feel good," Catherine said.

"Really? What do you mean?" Adeline stammered, her cheeks flushed with a mixture of shock and curiosity.

"Indeed, dear Adeline," Eliza replied with a mischievous grin, "one can experience an orgasm without the aid of a man."

"Is that so?" Adeline mused, her eyes wide with wonder. She couldn't fathom the idea of exploring such a realm of intimacy without the guiding tongue of Sir Alfred.

"Allow us to enlighten you," Amelia offered, her voice sultry and inviting. The other girls nodded in agreement, eager to share their knowledge with the innocent Adeline.

"First, you must find a comfortable and private space where you feel at ease," Catherine began, her authoritative tone softening as she spoke. "This is essential for allowing your body to fully relax and welcome new sensations."

Adeline's heart raced with anticipation as she listened intently, her mind painting vivid images of this newfound world of self-discovery.

"Next," Eliza continued, "you will explore your body with gentle touches, seeking out areas that elicit the strongest response."

As if guided by an unseen force, Adeline's hand timidly ventured beneath the layers of petticoats and skirts, hesitating slightly before making contact with her own skin. The sensation sent a shudder through her, both foreign and familiar at once.

"Take your time, dear," Amelia encouraged, her voice a soothing balm to Adeline's racing thoughts. "Allow yourself to truly savor each caress, and do not be afraid to experiment with different touches and pressures."

One by one, the girls began to disrobe, their movements slow and deliberate as they revealed their most intimate selves to one another. Although Adeline felt a fleeting moment of apprehension, the trust and camaraderie she shared with these young women emboldened her to follow suit.

All the laughter from just a few moments before was suddenly replaced with heavy breathing and soft moaning. The young women were touching themselves with wild abandon. Adeline watched them intently at first and then started touching herself too. The feeling was magical. While it wasn't the same as Sir Alfred's touch, it was definitely good enough.

Adeline's heart fluttered as she listened to the soft cooing of her new friends, the sound of their pleasure filling the air like a symphony. She quickly joined in with their chorus, her moans growing louder and more frequent as her excitement grew.

"I think I'm going to... I'm close..." Adeline panted, her thoughts turning to Sir Alfred and how he would make her climax.

"That's good, Adeline," Amelia sighed, her voice dripping with desire. "Let it happen. Just let it happen."

Adeline's legs began to quiver as she listened to the sensual symphony of her friends. Their voices mingled together in a pleasurable chorus, their moans and grunts harmonizing in a symphony of pleasure.

"AHHHHH!"

Adeline's body shuddered violently as the waves of pleasure crashed over her. Her thighs shook as her muscles contracted and spasmed, her breath coming out in ragged gasps. It wasn't long until all of the girls followed suit.

The girls remained still for a moment, all breathing heavily and coming down from their own peaks of pleasure. Adeline's hand continued to move between her legs, the sensations still radiating through her like aftershocks from an earthquake.

"That felt amazing," she whispered, her face flushed with exhilaration.

"It really is quite a magical feeling," Eliza replied, her smile radiating warmth.

The girls gathered close together, smiling and giggling as they all basked in the warm glow of their shared orgasms. Adeline had never felt so close to another group of girls.

5

The sun was setting over Hartfordshire Academy, casting a warm and golden glow upon the ivy-covered walls of the venerable institution. Sir Alfred, the esteemed headmaster, stood before his class of eager young ladies, a grave expression etched upon his noble visage. He cleared his throat, drawing their rapt attention to him as he prepared to deliver his news.

"Girls, I have some unfortunate tidings," he began, his voice somber. "Due to a pressing personal matter, I must take my leave of you for a short time, not more than a fortnight."

A murmur of dismay rippled through the assembly, eyes widening and hands clutching at skirts in consternation. Unbeknownst to the young ladies, the absence of Sir Alfred's guiding hand would awaken within them an insatiable hunger for the forbidden pleasures he had so diligently taught them.

"Please, Sir Alfred," cried Adeline, her delicate face the very picture of innocence, "who will supervise our education in your stead?"

"Alas, my dear Adeline, there is no one else with the requisite knowledge and expertise that I possess," Sir Alfred sighed. "You must endeavor to continue your studies on your own during my absence. I trust you all to behave in a manner befitting the reputation of Hartfordshire Academy."

With that, he took his leave of the classroom, the door closing behind him with an air of finality. The girls exchanged apprehensive glances, acutely aware of the void left by their beloved instructor.

In the days that followed, the once orderly halls of Hartfordshire Academy echoed with whispers of frustration and longing. The girls found themselves increasingly consumed by thoughts of the intimate lessons Sir Alfred had imparted, unable to shake their growing restlessness.

"Adeline, I cannot bear it any longer," confessed Rosamund, her pretty features flushed with desire. "I find myself longing for the touch of another, even as we practice our lessons alone."

"Indeed, dear Rosamund," Adeline replied, her own cheeks tinged with a rosy hue. "Our solitary exercises do little to quench the fire that burns within me."

Thus, in the secluded privacy of their dormitory, the young ladies began to engage in mutual masturbation sessions, seeking solace in one another's company as they attempted to satisfy their burgeoning desires. Yet even these intimate gatherings proved insufficient to assuage their insistent cravings.

"Adeline, I fear this is not enough," whispered Rosamund one evening, her eyes glistening with unshed tears of frustration. "We need guidance, the firm hand of Sir Alfred to show us the way."

"Patience, sweet Rosamund," Adeline murmured, her heart aching at her friend's distress. "Sir Alfred shall return to us soon, and all will be as it was before."

But as the days dragged on, the girls' desperation mounted, their shared experiences only serving to heighten their longing for something more. They could only hope that Sir Alfred would return to them swiftly, his skilled tutelage the key to unlocking the mysteries of their eager, unfulfilled bodies.

Under the dim glow of a single candle, the shadows danced upon the walls of Adeline's dormitory. The air was thick with anticipation, as Adeline and her friend, Isabella, sat on the edge of the bed, their hearts pounding in their chests.

"Adeline, are you certain we should proceed?" Isabella whispered, her voice quivering with anxiety. "What if we are discovered?"

"Trust me, Isabella," Adeline reassured her, taking her friend's delicate hand in hers. "Tonight, we shall attempt to find solace in one another's embrace."

With hesitant movements, Adeline drew Isabella close until their lips met in a tender kiss. The sensation of Isabella's warm breath mingling with hers sent shivers down Adeline's spine – a pleasant shock that intensified as Isabella's tongue tentatively ventured between them.

"Adeline..." Isabella murmured against her lips, the uncertainty in her voice slowly replaced by curiosity. "How do you feel?"

"Exhilarated," she confessed, her heart racing as she continued to explore the uncharted territory of her friend's mouth. "I've never dared to dream of such pleasure before."

"Nor I," admitted Isabella, her cheeks flushed with desire. "Shall we continue our exploration?"

"Indeed, let us venture further into this delightful abyss," Adeline agreed, emboldened by her friend's enthusiasm.

As they resumed their intimate exchange, Adeline allowed her fingers to trace the outline of Isabella's curves beneath the thin fabric of her nightgown. She marveled at the softness of Isabella's skin, the warmth radiating from her body.

"Adeline, your touch is... divine," Isabella sighed, her eyes fluttering closed as Adeline's fingertips danced across her chest, teasing the hardened peaks of her nipples.

"Tell me, Isabella, do you like this?" Adeline inquired, her own arousal growing with each breathy moan that escaped her friend's lips.

"More than I could have ever imagined," Isabella gasped, her voice trembling with desire.

Buoyed by Isabella's response, Adeline ventured further south, her hand slipping beneath the hem of her friend's nightgown. A silent plea passed between them as their eyes locked, and with a nod, Isabella granted Adeline permission to delve into the hidden depths of her womanhood.

As her fingers brushed against the slick warmth between Isabella's thighs, Adeline marveled at the delicate folds that seemed to beckon her closer. She felt a sense of awe and wonder at this most intimate connection, and as she began to carefully explore, Isabella's cries of pleasure grew louder, echoing through the chamber.

"Adeline, please... don't stop," Isabella begged, her body writhing beneath her friend's skillful touch.

"Never, dear Isabella," Adeline whispered, her own desire burning brighter than ever.

"Together, we will see to it that your needs are met."

The two young ladies quickly shed their nightclothes until they were both bare before one another. Adeline trembled as she observed the delicate contours of her friend's body, the curve of her hips and the swell of her breasts. Her own naked form was no less appealing to Isabella, who admired the fullness of Adeline's breasts and the gentle swell of her abdomen.

"You are truly beautiful, Adeline," Isabella murmured, her eyes glistening with emotion.

"Not half as lovely as you," Adeline replied, her slender fingers reaching out to trace the outline of her friend's rosy nipples.

"Please, Adeline, I beg of you – show me the rest," Isabella implored, her hand moving to cover Adeline's.

With a nervous nod, Adeline gently guided Isabella's hand down to her most intimate region, her breath catching in her throat as she felt her friend's delicate fingers brush against her folds.

As her fingers slid inside Isabella's slick depths, Adeline felt her own body pulse in time with her friend's, the raw arousal surging between their bodies like a raging inferno.

Isabella's fingers moved to gently brush against Adeline's clit and then plunged deep into her vagina, eliciting a strangled moan from her lips as the two young women continued their intimate explorations.

"Again... Isabella, please," Adeline begged, her fingers pumping in and out of her friend's slick pussy. "I need more."

Beneath her touch, Isabella's body quivered with delight, her hips bucking against Adeline's relentless fingers. Before long, the two young women had ascended to new heights of pleasure, their bodies growing feverish with each passing moment.

"I feel as though I am floating, Adeline," Isabella gasped as a powerful orgasm rippled through her body, bringing her to new heights of ecstasy. "Am I dreaming?"

"I cannot say," Adeline replied, her heart pounding in her chest as she felt the warm flood of Isabella's juices coat her hand.

As they basked in the throes of their mutual orgasm, Isabella and Adeline's eyes locked, delirium fueling their lustful gazes. Then, with the heat of passion still coursing through their veins, the two young women slowly collapsed in each others' arms, their thoughts consumed with feverish visions of one another.

"Isabella... I fear there is one last step," Adeline murmured, her hand gently brushing the soft locks of her friend's hair.

"Tell me, Adeline," Isabella replied, her heart pounding in her chest. "Whatever it is, I will do it for you."

"With your guidance, we must delve further into this most delicate matter," Adeline explained, her cheeks flushed with anticipation. "I fear that I cannot resist my urges for much longer."

"Then come closer, my dear Adeline," Isabella whispered, her eyes twinkling with the promise of forbidden pleasures.

In the soft light of the moon, Isabella spread her legs, drawing Adeline's head closer to her glistening pussy. Adeline's heart pounded in her chest as she gently parted Isabella's delicate folds, moving her tongue to slowly trace the outline of her clit.

"Adeline... please," Isabella begged, her body twitching in anticipation.

Slowly, Adeline's tongue continued its exploration of Isabella's pussy, each flick of her tongue bringing her friend closer and closer to orgasm. At last, Adeline flicked her tongue against Isabella's throbbing clit, watching with delight as her friend's body tensed, her entire being consumed with ecstasy.

"I'm cumming... Adeline!" Isabella cried out, her body shuddering as sensation after sensation washed over her.

A great sense of fulfillment washed over Adeline as she felt her friend's juices coat her tongue, her body aching for her own release. Unable to contain herself, Adeline slid her hand between her legs, her fingers quickly finding the aching bud of her clit.

"Oh, Isabella, watch me," Adeline moaned, her fingers rapidly working up and down the length of her pussy.

As Isabella watched, Adeline's entire body quaked as she neared the brink of ecstasy. And then, with a final cry of pleasure, the two young women's bodies erupted together, their cries of ecstasy echoing through the night.

For a few moments, the two young women lay in each others' arms, their breathing slowly returning to normal. Then, with a smile upon her face, Adeline leaned in to kiss her new lover.

"Thank you for sharing this moment with me," Isabella replied, her cheeks rosy with pleasure. "I will never forget this night."

6

A few days later, Sir Alfred returned to Hartfordshire Academy and the girls were all eager to resume their lessons. On his first night back, Alfred summoned Adeline to his study. She was to be the first to start her studies back up.

"Come in, child," his voice rumbled from within.

Adeline entered, clutching her dressing gown tight. Sir Alfred stood by the fireplace, glass of brandy in hand, silhouetted by the flickering flames.

"Do you know why I've called you here?"

She swallowed. "Yes, sir."

"And are you prepared to become a woman?"

Her cheeks flushed hot. She thought of the lessons, the touches, the aching desire he'd awakened within her. She nodded.

Sir Alfred strode toward her. "Speak, girl. I won't have a mute for a lover.

"Yes, sir. I'm ready," she whispered.

He cupped her chin, gazing into her eyes. "Good. Now, remove your gown and get on the bed."

Her hands shook as she untied the sash and let the gown fall to the floor. Naked, she climbed onto the bed as ordered.

Sir Alfred began removing his jacket, his eyes raking over her exposed body. Adeline's heart threatened to burst from her chest. So many emotions warred within her—anticipation, excitement. She was so ready for this.

He sat on the edge of the bed and ran a hand up her leg. "Lovely. You'll make a fine woman yet, my dear."

His touch ignited fire in her veins. She was ready, so ready to feel his cock inside her.

"I won't be gentle," he warned. "But you will enjoy every moment."

Adeline breathed deep, summoning her courage. She spread her legs. "I am yours, sir. Do with me as you will."

Sir Alfred began kissing and licking Adeline's thighs, like a starving man being presented with his first meal in days. He quickly made his way to her pussy which was already dripping wet.

"You are ready, aren't you? You want my cock?"

"Yes, sir."

Alfred smiled and rolled her onto her stomach. He spread her legs and positioned himself behind her. He caressed her back and buttocks, then his fingers trailed down toward her pussy.

"I'm going to make you scream, my dear."

"Yes, yes," she said, breathlessly. "I want your cock, sir."

Adeline felt the violent trembling of his cock against her backside and the heat of his breath in her ear. She stiffened as his cock pressed against her pussy, and she gasped as it slid inside her. Alfred drew back, then rammed forward again, filling her completely. Adeline cried out as his cock pounded her pussy. His hands clenched her hips, holding her in place, as he thrust again and again. She could feel every ridge and vein of his cock as it thrust into her tender flesh. A stabbing, burning pain began to radiate from her pussy all through her body as he fucked her.

"Oh, god, fuck me!"

The pain began to dissipate and was replaced by another sensation. It started at her pussy, then spread throughout her body. Her pussy was on fire, her clit throbbed. She cried out as wave after wave of pleasure overtook her.

He rammed her harder, faster. The headboard smashed against the wall as he fucked her harder still. She could feel his cock throbbing, the head expanding. His breath was ragged, his cock shoving harder and harder as he neared orgasm. He pulled her hair, her head snapping back and she screamed as her pussy convulsed and shuddered, spewing out a hot gush of juices. Her eyes rolled back in her head as a powerful orgasm shook her from head to toe.

He pulled his cock from her with a wet sucking sound and she collapsed on the bed, spent.

Alfred stood and moved away from the bed. She turned and saw him stroking his cock. "You will suck, now," he demanded.

Adeline turned and crawled to him on hands and knees. She was surprised to realize that her clit was still throbbing from the powerful orgasm she'd had. She took his cock and licked and sucked at it with eager delight.

Sir Alfred's knees buckled and he nearly collapsed. He gripped her hair and slammed his cock into her mouth, pumping it in and out of her mouth. Her hands grabbed at his buttocks to keep her from falling.

Her eyes widened as she felt the first hot gush of his cum hit the back of her throat. It was salty and smelled faintly of brandy. Another rush of cum flooded her mouth and she swallowed as fast as she could to keep it from overflowing. She sucked and stroked with her tongue, wanting to taste every drop.

Another blast of his cum hit her mouth she tried to swallow it but some spilled out and dribbled down her chin.

Sir Alfred gasped for breath, his cock finally spent. He pulled out of her mouth and fell back against the wall.

"Oh, my dear," he moaned. "You are a wench indeed."

Adeline crawled back to the bed. She licked the cum from her lips and chin, trying to get every last drop. Her pussy still throbbed.

She sat up and looked at Sir Alfred. "I want to know. Was that well done?"

Sir Alfred turned his head and grinned at her. His cock was still hard. "You are a natural," he said. "But I have more to teach you."

"Lie back down," Alfred ordered.

When she did, he climbed onto the bed, his cock in his hand. He spread her legs, then rammed his cock into her pussy. Adeline's head flew back and she clutched at the bed sheets, whimpering.

As Sir Alfred fucked her, his cock grew and Adeline's pussy became wetter than it had been before. Her whole body felt on fire as he fucked her. She gasped as his cock slammed into her pussy and then cried out as another orgasm overwhelmed her.

Sir Alfred's cock expanded, throbbing, then he pulled his cock out of her pussy and began to stroke it.

The next instant cum erupted from his cock, blasting Adeline's stomach and breasts. Cum splattered across her face and trickled down, then pooled in her navel. When Alfred was finished, he was no longer hard, but his cock still leaked more cum.

She smiled and slid down on the bed, then pulled Sir Alfred's cock into her mouth. She licked and sucked at his cock, swallowing the cum as fast as she could. She was hot, her pussy throbbed, and she wanted to make him hard again.

She stroked his cock while she licked the cum from it. Her touch brought it back to life and a moan escaped Alfred's mouth. She began to lick and suck his cock with more urgency and it stiffened. His cock grew larger again, bigger than Adeline thought possible.

"Oh, you are a greedy wench, aren't you?" he moaned, his eyes closed.

"I want you again," she said. "I want to make you cum."

Sir Alfred's eyes flew open and he looked down at her. "You are quite the student, aren't you?"

Adeline kissed his cock. "I want to know, sir."

He laughed. "You will, my dear. You will."

He fucked her again and again that night, teaching her how to suck his cock, then her cunt. When his cock was hard, he fucked her, then when it was soft, he sucked her pussy. When he was finally done with her, Sir Alfred left her sleeping on the bed.

Adeline was exhausted but she was also elated. She had done it. She had given herself to him completely. She had allowed him to fuck her and she had pleased him. She dreamed that night of what it would be like when she became a proper woman.

In the morning, she woke to find herself sore and bruised, but she was happy. She lay in bed and thought of Sir Alfred. He was kind, she knew that, but he was also demanding. She thought of his cock, massive and hard, and of his mouth on her pussy, and she felt a thrill rush through her. She couldn't wait to find out what was next.

7

The sun dipped behind the horizon, casting a golden glow on the grand drawing room of Hartfordshire Academy. Adeline stood with her classmates, their eyes fixed on Sir Alfred as he prepared to address them. She twirled a strand of her chestnut hair around her finger, feeling both trepidation and excitement course through her veins.

"Girls," Sir Alfred began, his voice commanding attention, "as you know, our esteemed Adeline has joined you and recently completed what was required of her, and thus it is time for us to move towards the last stage in your education. Your final exam."

He paused, surveying the room filled with attentive young women dressed in delicate lace gowns. Adeline's heart fluttered; she had heard whispers of this final portion of their studies but knew not what it entailed.

"You will be tested. You will be tasked with pleasing other gentlemen – those who have been carefully chosen by me for their fine qualities and upstanding reputations." Sir Alfred declared, a hint of pride glinting in his eyes.

Adeline's cheeks flushed at the thought. Although she had just begun to explore the world of carnal pleasures, the idea of being intimate with someone other than Sir Alfred felt foreign and daunting.

"Rest assured, my dear girls," Sir Alfred continued, sensing their apprehension, "I have taken great care in selecting only the most suitable men for this phase of your education. They are all of good stock, well-mannered, and quite handsome, if I may say so myself."

A ripple of nervous laughter swept through the room. Adeline glanced at her peers, their eyes alight with curiosity and anticipation. The prospect of meeting these men sent a thrill down her spine, even as uncertainty gnawed at her.

"Your test will consist of pleasing these men to the best of your ability, ensuring that you leave Hartfordshire Academy as the most accomplished young ladies in all of England." Sir Alfred concluded, his words ringing with conviction.

Adeline drew a deep breath, her thoughts a whirlwind. She knew that she must trust in Sir Alfred's guidance, but the thought of pleasing other men seemed an insurmountable challenge. As her classmates chattered excitedly around her, she resolved to face the unknown with courage and grace, just as she had done so many times before within these walls.

"Your first test," Sir Alfred announced, "will be to demonstrate your prowess in the art of oral pleasure. The second test will require you to fully engage in the act of lovemaking. And finally, the third test is to submit to your partner's desires, ensuring his utmost satisfaction. Only upon successful completion of these tests shall you earn your place as graduates of Hartfordshire Academy."

Adeline felt a swell of anxiety within her chest, her heart pounding like the hooves of a wild stallion. She glanced around the room, catching the expressions on her classmates' faces - a mixture of excitement, fear, and determination.

"Remember, my dears," Sir Alfred added, his voice firm yet caring, "failure will result in being sent back to your families, bearing the weight of shame upon your shoulders."

As the days passed, Adeline found herself consumed by thoughts of the impending tests. She practiced her art with diligence and sought counsel from her peers, hoping to prepare for whatever challenges lay ahead.

On the fateful evening, the great hall of the academy was filled with the scent of fresh flowers and the soft glow of candlelight. A murmur of anticipation buzzed through the air as the girls lined up, dressed in their finest gowns, awaiting the arrival of their chosen partners.

"Adeline," Sir Alfred whispered, leaning close as he handed her a folded piece of paper, "you have been paired with Lord Charles Whitethorn."

"Thank you, Sir," she replied, her voice barely audible, her hands trembling as she accepted the paper.

The doors opened, revealing a group of impeccably dressed men who strode into the hall with an air of confidence. As they approached, Adeline spotted Lord Charles, his tall figure adorned in a fine black suit, his dark hair framing a handsome face that bore a warm smile.

"Miss Adeline," he greeted her, extending his hand with a slight bow.

"Lord Charles," she replied, placing her delicate hand in his as they exchanged formalities. His touch was gentle yet firm, and she found herself inexplicably drawn to him as they made their way to one of the many lavish bedrooms in the academy.

"Are you ready, my dear?" Lord Charles asked, his voice soft and soothing as they entered the dimly lit chamber.

Adeline hesitated, finding solace in the depths of his dark eyes, which seemed to promise safety and understanding. "I am," she whispered, steeling herself for the first test: oral sex.

As Lord Charles reclined on the plush bed, Adeline knelt before him, her heart thundering in her chest. This is it, she thought, I must prove myself worthy and pass these tests. There's no turning back now.

Adeline began by unfastening and pulling down Lord Charles' trousers. This was only the second cock she had ever seen. It wasn't quite as long as Sir Alfred's but it was even thicker than his. She was filled with amazement and couldn't wait to experience it.

"Do you like that?" Lord Charles asked.

"Yes sir. It's a most handsome cock."

Adeline kissed the tip of his cock and then slowly began to lick it from base to tip. His pre-cum dripped in her mouth and she loved how rich his cock tasted. She kept her lips softly locked around his cock and rubbed his shaft with her tongue while her hands stroked gently on his balls. The more she worked on his cock with her mouth the more pre-cum splurged from the tip.

"I want you to lick every bit of my cock clean," Lord Charles stated.

Adeline held Lord Charles' cock in both hands and began to suck on it as if it was a lollipop. She gave it all her best effort and managed to get all of his cock into her mouth. She worked on it so hard that he began to moan and his cock began twitching. After that she slowly drew out his cock and gave a few licks to the head, which made him groan even louder.

Adeline gave one last lick to his cock as it slowly twitched and began to shrivel. "I want you to cum in my mouth," she explained to him. Just as she said that, his erection began to throb. She opened her mouth as wide as she could and guided his cock back into it.

Adeline felt a warm rush of liquid fill her mouth and spill out onto her tongue. She eagerly swallowed his cum, but there was so much that it began to dribble out of her mouth and down his soft cock.

"That was very good, Adeline."

"Thank you, sir. I'm glad you enjoyed it."

"You can be sure that I will let Sir Alfred know that you passed the first test. I can't wait until tomorrow night when we move on to test two."

"I am very much looking forward to it, Lord Charles."

***

They cleaned up and dressed and made their way back downstairs. All of the couples were trickling in around the same time. Everyone seemed to be happy. I was hopeful that everyone passed test one. I didn't want to see any of my friends fail.

Sir Alfred joined them in the ballroom and asked each of the men one by one if their lady passed their test. One by one they each shouted a resounding yes. Everyone erupted in applause. What a relief!

Sir Alfred dismissed everyone with orders to come back tomorrow night for test two.

8

The next night, the men returned eagerly, their anticipation palpable as they gathered in the grand hall of Hartfordshire Academy. Sir Alfred stood at the front of the room, his eyes dark and commanding as he surveyed the assembled group. He smiled, a predatory gleam in his eyes as he addressed them. "Well done, gentlemen. The girls performed admirably last night. Tonight, we take it to the next level."

A collective gasp rippled through the crowd as he continued. "You are to engage in full on fucking with the same girls you had the night before. You have one hour."

The room erupted into a cacophony of excited chatter and eager moans, the air thick with lust and desire. The girls, lined up and looked on with hungry eyes, their hands gently caressing themselves in anticipation of what was to come. The men were led in, one by one, to find their partners. Some paused to kiss and grope their chosen girl before leading them upstairs to the dormitories.

Adeline and Lord Charles quickly made their way to their

room. Adeline was unsure what to expect tonight. But she knew she wanted very badly to please Lord Charles.

After entering the room, Lord Charles commanded Adeline to take her clothes off, which she did. He watched her with intense desire, practically drooling at the site of her swollen breasts and pink pussy. Adeline was a little taken aback by the intensity of his stare. He looked like a ravenous dog being presented with his first meal in weeks.

Lord Charles told Adeline to lie down on the bed. As she lay back on the creaky wooden slat-frame bed, her fingers traced circles around her swollen pussy. She wanted his desire to be stronger than ever. Lord Charles watched her carefully as he began to undress. His cock was already hard as a rock. Adeline licked her lips as he approached the bed, her heart racing with excitement.

He roughly pushed her legs apart and positioned his face between them. He immediately began licking her pussy with a fervor that sent shivers down Adeline's spine. His tongue flicked and danced across her sensitive clit, his lips sucking and nibbling, driving her to the brink of ecstasy. Adeline moaned, the sound mingling with the wet sounds of their passion filling the room.

Lord Charles was relentless in his pursuit of pleasuring Adeline. His skilled tongue explored every inch of her dripping core, his fingers plunging into her depths, matching the rhythm of his oral assault. Adeline arched her back and gripped the bedsheets, her body trembling with pleasure.

As Lord Charles continued to devour her with an insatiable hunger, Adeline's thoughts became consumed by a wild desire to have his cock inside her.

"Fuck me, Lord Charles," she begged.

"You want me to fuck you? Your wish is my command."

"Now be a good girl," he growled before slamming into her with a force that made her gasp.

Her pussy stretched and ached around the thickness of his cock, filling her up completely as he began to pound into her in a rhythm that was both brutal and exhilarating. The headboard thudded against the wall with every thrust, the sound echoing through the room. Moans and grunts filled the air as they fucked like animals, their need for release palpable. His hands dug into her shoulders, leaving bruises from the force of his grip. She clawed at the sheets, arching her back in pleasure as he took her hard.

He pulled her hair, forcing her head back, exposing her neck as he bit down, leaving a bruise there. "Take it like a whore," he hissed into her ear.

She whimpered, her eyes rolling back into her head as she felt a rush of endorphins washing over her. Her body tensed and released with each powerful stroke, the sensation almost too much to bear. The room reeked of sweat and sex, the air heavy with arousal. They were completely lost in each other, oblivious to everything but the primal urge to cum.

His hips slammed into hers one last time, sending her careening over the edge. Her body convulsed around his cock, milking his release as he groaned her name and filled her with his hot seed. She came with a scream, her pussy clenching tightly around him as she shuddered in ecstasy. The room fell silent except for their ragged breathing and the sound of their hearts pounding in unison.

In the aftermath, they collapsed into each other's arms, their sweaty bodies sticky with sweat and each other's fluids. They lay entwined, eyes locked on each other's, their chests rising and falling rapidly. It was a moment that would be forever etched into her mind as she whispered, "That was... amazing."

He chuckled darkly. "It's only the beginning, my dear." He kissed her passionately, his tongue dancing with hers.

"I want you again." She murmured hoarsely.

"You shall have me, Adeline," He growled, rolling off of her and onto his back. He panted heavily, his chest heaving as he stared up at the ceiling.

She crawled over him, her round, perfect breasts swaying enticingly as she straddled his hips. She lowered herself down onto him, taking him deep inside of her again, moaning softly at the feeling of being filled so completely. He gripped her hips, guiding her up and down, their eyes locked on one another as they began to move together in a sensual rhythm.

His fingers dug into her shoulders. She cried out in pleasure, her nails raking down his chest as she rode him hard. They were both lost in the blissful agony of their desires, completely consumed by the lust that threatened to overwhelm them. She wrapped her legs around him, feeling the rough skin of his thighs against her sensitive inner thighs.

Their sex became rougher, more urgent, their bodies moving together like two animals in heat. He groaned loudly as he felt her tighten around him, ready to cum again. He pushed into her just right, hitting that spot that made her scream out his name, her walls clenching around him. Her juices flowed down his shaft, making it slick and hot.

Finally spent, they collapsed onto the bed together, panting heavily.

After a short time passed, they realized that their hour was almost up. They quickly got up and dressed and made their way back down to the ballroom where the others were also slowly trickling in, in various states of bliss.

Sir Alfred addressed them all. "Alright gentlemen, you've had an hour for these ladies to provide you with a thorough fucking. How did they handle it?"

One by one, they stepped forward, declaring their satisfaction, making sure to mention her name. Lord Charles waited for his turn, not taking his eyes off of Adeline.

"Adeline was incredible," he said, a smile on his face. "She never failed to please me."

9

The men arrived back on the third night, their faces hungry and eager as they took in their surroundings. All the ladies were present, standing or kneeling in the grandiose ballroom, wearing the most revealing lingerie and costumes possible.

The scent of arousal and anticipation hung heavy in the air, an aphrodisiac that made Sir Alfred grin wickedly as he addressed them.

"Gentlemen, I trust you've enjoyed yourselves thus far. Tonight, you have the entire night. Do as you wish with the ladies."

There were murmurs of excitement from the assembled group as they eyed the shapely forms before them, waiting to be taken in hand. Many of the couples decided not to even wait until they got to their rooms and instead immediately began tearing into each other right there in the ballroom. Sir Alfred stepped back and allowed them to move forward, and the first gentleman to approach his chosen lady grabbed her wrist roughly and pulled her to him, roughly kissing her neck before pushing her down to her knees. His cock sprung free from his trousers, and she obediently took it into her mouth, sucking eagerly as he roughly thrust into her. Another man grabbed the breast of his lady, roughly pinching a nipple before taking her roughly against the wall and thrusting into her, the force of his hips sending a moan from her lips as she gripped his shoulders tightly.

A third gentleman caressed his lady's cheek before lowering his face to hers, his tongue exploring her mouth deeply as his hand trailed down to rub against her core, already damp with desire. She purred in response, arching her back for more contact.

Across the room, a fourth man pushed his lady onto a nearby table and lifted her skirts, exposing her undergarments. His hand gripped her thigh, his thumb finding its way between the crotch of her panties and rubbing against her clit as she gasped. He took her breast roughly in his mouth, sucking hard on the perky nipple as he fingered her, pushing harder against her sensitive bud.

The ladies moaned and whimpered in unison, their eyes rolling back in ecstasy as they were taken by their masters. The air was heavy with the scent of arousal and desire, pierced by gasps and groans of pure pleasure.

Sir Alfred looked on, his eyes gleaming with satisfaction. This was exactly what he had hoped for. These individuals were truly living out their deepest desires in this secretive academy, away from prying eyes. He took a step back to observe from the shadows, watching as one gentleman tore at his lady's clothing, exposing her delicate skin to the cool air of the ballroom. Another lifted her by her hair, forcing her to meet his gaze as he thrust into her from behind, her cries of pleasure muffled by his powerful grip.

In another corner, a lady was bent over a table, her bottom raised invitingly in the air as a gentleman spanked her red bottom, leaving a fiery sting that only turned her on more. She spread her legs wide, offering herself to him as he pressed his hard length against her wet folds.

Adeline was amazed and aroused by what she saw. But Lord Charles had other plans. They made their way to their room. She was in a daze, the sights and sounds still playing out on her mind's canvas as they entered the opulent chamber. She couldn't help but notice the unusual setup - ropes hanging from the ceiling, whips scattered across the bed, strange devices on the dresser. Her heart raced as she took it all in.

"Close your eyes, Adeline," commanded Lord Charles, his voice low and seductive. He wanted to see her reaction when she discovered the many surprises he had in store for her. Without hesitation, she complied.

Her hands fumbled behind her back, feeling the cool silk of the blindfold being tied around her head. Suddenly, she was in complete darkness. "Now," he purred, "open your mouth." His hard cock was pressed against her lips, and she obeyed, taking it inside her mouth. The taste was enticing, making her mouth water.

"Swirl your tongue," he ordered, and she did as she was told, feeling him grow harder against her tongue.

A rustle of fabric and she felt him unfastening her corset. It fell away, leaving her breasts bare and free, nipples hard from both anticipation and fear. She gasped when icy cold metal clinked against them, followed by the tug of a chain between them. Another gasp escaped her when he slipped something thick and throbbing between her lips and teased her entrance before pushing inside her.

"What is this?" she asked, feeling full yet achingly empty.

"A dildo," he grunted.

His hands roamed down her stomach, caressing her skin before slipping lower, causing her to shiver at the contact.

"This," he said, his voice rough with desire, "is your first lesson in submission, Adeline. You belong to me now." His words sent shivers down her spine.

Bound and helpless, she could only wait for his next move.

The room filled with the sound of leather striking flesh - his hand on her ass cheek. He growled low as he spanked her, leaving a hot sting that drove her wild. Each smack echoed through the room like thunder, making her pussy clench around the toy inside her. He laughed darkly and continued, pushing her boundaries further than she'd ever imagined possible.

"Now," he said, his voice low and husky, "you can taste yourself." And she did, licking her juices from his fingers like they were the sweetest nectar.

Her breathing labored, she felt him unfastening the ropes that bound her wrists. He took hold of her hands and guided them above her head, tying them securely once again.

"Spread your legs wider," he ordered, and she complied, feeling the weight of the chains pulling at her wrists.

As he pushed his cock against her entrance, she knew there was no going back. Their hips grinding together created music that filled the room.

"You are mine," he whispered, sliding in fully, claiming her with each deep thrust. Their eyes locked as they moved in perfect rhythm, lost in the heat of their lustful dance.

She sobbed his name, feeling fulfilled and used in ways she never thought possible, as he gave her what she had always craved... control.

Lord Charles's thrusts became harder, faster, like he couldn't get enough of her. She felt the headboard hitting the wall with each powerful stroke and welcomed the pain that came with it, demanding more. Adeline screamed out in pleasure as she felt him hit her G-spot time and again. Her body shook with orgasm after orgasm, each wave crashing over her like the most intense tide.

After they'd both found release, they collapsed in a pile of sweaty limbs and spent desire. Lord Charles rested his forehead against hers, breathing heavily, their bond stronger than ever. He looked into her eyes, his gaze unwavering.

"That... was just the beginning," he promised.

Soon after, there was a knock on the door and in walked several other couples.

"Can we join in now?" one man asked.

Hours passed in a blur of ecstasy and desire as the other couples joined in, creating a writhing mass of naked limbs and hungry mouths. Adeline found herself being passed from one pair of hands to the next, feeling both used and cherished at the same time. Lips trailed fire across her skin, teeth grazed her nipples, and fingers found every hidden crevice. She moaned and whimpered, begging for more as they showed her the depths of their depravity.

One woman knelt between her legs, licking at her folds while another man fucked her from behind. Her cries of pleasure filled the room, echoing off the walls.

"You're such a dirty little slut," the woman said, laughing as she pushed two fingers deep inside Adeline's ass. "But you take it like a champ."

A man brought out a riding crop and began to strike Adeline's over-sensitized skin, leaving red marks behind. She cried out in pain-tinged ecstasy, her body arching towards it.

"Please, sir... more."

Finally, Lord Charles stood before her, his cock hard once again. He bound her hands above her head, blindfolding her as well. She shivered in anticipation, knowing he would take her in ways she'd never imagined. A cool sensation spread across her ass as he smoothed lubricant over it.

"Ready for your first anal training, my dear?" he whispered in her ear.

Adeline nodded, unable to form words. He pushed in slowly, filling her completely, causing her to groan around the gag in her mouth. With each thrust, she felt more of him filling her, stretching her. It hurt but it felt so good, so right.

"You're mine now," he growled, slapping her ass lightly.

Soon enough, they were locked in their own private dance of lust, their bodies moving in perfect sync as they found release again and again. Adeline couldn't believe how intensely she craved this feeling - how much she needed it. She hadn't known what she was missing until now.

As dawn broke, they all collapsed, sweaty and satiated. Adeline looked around at the tangled mass of limbs, feeling both exhausted and strangely fulfilled.

Sir Alfred watched as the couples returned to the ballroom, their faces flushed and dewy from their intense fucking. He smiled broadly, pleased with the results.

One by one he asked the gentlemen if their ladies pleased them in this final sexual test. The gentlemen were all eager to praise the young women.

Sir Alfred's eyes gleamed with satisfaction as he listened to the gentlemen sing praises of their ladies' performance in the final sexual test. It was a carefully crafted experiment, designed to assess not only the physical prowess of the women but also their ability to please and satisfy their partners.

As each gentleman shared his thoughts, Sir Alfred felt a surge of pride. His meticulous training and preparation had paid off. The women he had selected for this exceptional gathering were no ordinary maidens; they were handpicked for their beauty, charm, and innate sensuality.

The ballroom was adorned with opulent decorations, reflecting the luxurious nature of the event. The air was thick with lingering desire, mingling with the scent of expensive perfumes and freshly moistened skin. Sir Alfred knew that this night would be talked about for years to come, whispered among those who craved such illicit pleasures.

With a voice that carried authority and grace, Sir Alfred addressed the crowd. "Ladies and gentlemen, I am overwhelmed by the success of this evening's festivities. It is with great pleasure that I announce the results of this three-part sexual test." The room erupted with applause and whispers of anticipation. Sir Alfred continued, his voice filled with admiration.

"Now," Sir Alfred continued, his eyes sparkling mischievously, "for the ladies. Each one of you has exhibited extraordinary talent and skill in pleasuring your partners. Your dedication to your studies here at Hartfordshire Academy is truly commendable and I am honored to have witnessed your journeys. And with that I say that you have all passed and have graduated with honors."

As the room continued to buzz with excitement, Lord Charles pulled Adeline aside.

"Adeline, you have impressed me greatly with your beauty, your charm, and your ability to satisfy me sexually. I would very much like it if you came back with me to Whitethorne Manor to live a life of pleasure and adventure. You will have everything you ever wanted and more."

Adeline's heart fluttered at Lord Charles' proposition. She had dreamed of what life would be like beyond the confines of Hartfordshire Academy, a life where she could explore her desires and passions freely. The thought of being whisked away to WhitethorneManor, where pleasure and adventure awaited her, ignited a fire within her.

She looked into Lord Charles' eyes, searching for any sign of deceit or insincerity. But all she found was an intense gaze filled with desire and longing. It was a look that spoke volumes, promising her a life of fulfillment and excitement.

A smile tugged at the corners of Adeline's lips as she nodded in acceptance. "Lord Charles, I cannot deny the pull I feel towards you. Your offer is more than tempting, and I would be honored to join you at Whitethorne Manor."

Lord Charles' face lit up with delight, his hand caressing Adeline's cheek tenderly. "My dear Adeline, you have made me the happiest man tonight with your acceptance. I promise you, life at Whitethorne Manor will be unlike anything you have ever experienced."

Adeline's heart raced as Lord Charles leaned in, his lips brushing against hers in a gentle, intoxicating kiss. It was a promise sealed with the taste of desire and an undeniable connection that left her breathless. In that moment, she knew she had made the right choice.

THE END